Of Doors and Betrayal

A. Carys

A. Carys

The characters and events portrayed in this book are fictitious. Any similarity to real persons, living or dead, is coincidental and not intended by the author.

No part of this book may be reproduced, or stored in a retrieval system, or transmitted in any form or by any means, electronic, mechanical, photocopying, recording, or otherwise, without express written permission of the publisher.

Copyright © 2024 A. Carys

All rights reserved.

BOOKS IN THIS SERIES

Of Doors and Betrayal

The Pickpocket and the Princess

The Master, My Wings, Our Service

'Cos This Is How Villains Are Made

A Circus of Wonder

A Sentence to Death

A Deal With The Devil

Let Her Go

The Three

Queen Rory, The Banished

A. Carys

Of Doors and Betrayal

DEDICATION

I can do anything if I believe in myself.

gulps

A. Carys

CHAPTER ONE

I've always wondered what the stars would look like up close.

Would they be shimmery, as though they've been covered in glitter?

Or would they be intricately detailed with rivets and mini craters?

But those seem like a small and menial questions while I lay upon a cloud, directly underneath a half-formed planet. Red veins spiral out from the centre as it weaves itself together. A planet being born right in front of my eyes. Admiring this natural, or unnatural, creation is the only thing I can do right now.

I can't run. I can't sit up.

I can't move.

All I can do is wonder what death will feel like.

Will it envelope me in warmth and rays of light as I pass? Or will it drape me with a cool breeze, stopping just overhead until I take my final breath?

I can't even cry out, being one of the Inhumans means I'm mute. One of ten thousand mutes on the planet. While I can't make noise, though I hope the lord knows I want to, my transmitter gasps and stutters. It beeps like a heart monitor, reassuring me that I'm still alive.

I struggle to lift my hands, both of them feeling like they've been strapped with weights. After much struggling, my hands finally touch. I flex my fingers and they weakly press the red button on the side. It flashes red as it sends back my call sign.

The Rebellion won't reach me in time, but at least they'll know. At least they'll know that something happened to me.

TRANSMISSION: MAYDAY

TRANSMISSION: M-MAYDAY

At least I know I'll get a headstone.

TRANSMISSION: MAYDA-AY

TRANSMISSION: MAYDAY-DAY

I feel my heartbeat slow down. It stutters and palpitates as my breath catches in my throat. My stomach hurts, everything aches and the monitor flatlines.

One breath…

Two breath..

Three breath.

A. Carys

TRANSCRIPT OF KERES EDIM FINAL CONTACT WITH BASE

KERES EDIM'S TRANSMITTER - KERES EDIM TRANSMITTER AND MONITOR DETECTED SIGNS OF LIFE CEASED AT 0303 PM.

BASE - UNDERSTOOD AND RECEIVED, TRANSMITTER TO CONFIRM LOCATION FOR IMMEDIATE RECOVERY, TEAM DISPATCHED.

KERES EDIM'S TRANSMITTER - LOCATION, UN-UN-UNKNOWN. LOCATION UNKNOWN.

BASE - LOCATION NOTED AS UNKNOWN, WE'RE ATTEMPTING A TRACE NOW.

KERES EDIM'S TRANSMITTER - UNK-UNKNOWN. TRANSMITTER BAT-BATTERY LOW.

BASE - REPEAT, ATTEMPTING A TRACE NOW. BASE REQUESTING LOCATION DATA FROM TRANSMITTER

KERES EDIM'S TRANSMITTER - TRANSMITTER BAT-BAT-BATTERY LO-

CHAPTER TWO

Four days earlier...

Wandering the halls of the underground base, I wonder who will get the next assignment, the Observatory Aerimar assignment. Apparently, it'll be a career changer.

I squeeze through the gaps of the crowd the has gathered around the meeting table. Everyone who is available for field duty has come to find out if they are the lucky person.

Amy, Leader of the Haroval Rebellion, stands on the other side of the table. The one person around here that has any kind of say over anything. The only person who can give orders and the only person who can give out assignments.

This base, Amy's base, runs on Aerimar stones. They're a strong power source that helps keep the lights on now that the Higher Power has cut off electricity and heat to the lower districts in the south. He was hoping to flush us out and into his awaiting army circle, but we burrowed underground. Into the safety of the tunnel system that took Amy seven years to construct. Ever since she began to sense the rising tensions in the Capital, she took extreme precautions to ensure the safety of both the movement and the people involved.

"Good afternoon, everyone. Nice to see how eager all of you are to take on this job."

Cheers resound around the room.

"There's only one place on this job to be given out. That person will be sent into the Observatory to retrieve a box of Aerimar stones. It's a high-risk assignment since the increase in protection around public buildings, but it will be heavily rewarding if the person is successful."

"So, who have you picked?" shouts someone in the crowd.

Everyone chuckles.

"Keres Edim," she announces as she pulls my picture up on the holo-monitor. "You've been working very hard as of late and have made significant progress in all areas of your training. The assignment is yours if you choose to accept it."

Amy looks directly at me, smiling as she awaits my answer. I nod, furiously. My transmitter beeps, *"Yes."*

I can't actually talk. I wish I could, but my family tree is deeply woven with the mutation gene that was forced upon thousands of people over five hundred years ago. Everyone in my family, along with hundreds of other families, are mute as well. The transmitters speak for us, they're hard wired into the part of the brain that is responsible for our thoughts. It transforms them into words so that we can have normal conversations with others.
It's a more recent technology, so not everyone has one yet. But those who do, have found them to be extremely useful.

"Good. Report to my office tomorrow morning at 9 am."

I nod, smiling. People around me congratulate

me. They pat me on the back and wish me good luck. I nod with thanks as Amy carries on speaking, taking us through the rest of the assignments up for grabs. She finishes the meeting by showing us the progress we've made with getting spies into key places around the country. Places such as the palace, all of the churches and the parliamentary building where the Higher Power holds important meetings with his investors and followers.

It takes a while for everyone to file out of the room, but when I manage to squeeze through a gap in the crowd, someone grabs my arm and drags me away. I instantly know who has hold of me, Jonah Koll. I will never know what I did to make him hate me, but he makes everything a competition and constantly tries to put me down. So I can only imagine the anger coursing through him at the fact that I was given the assignment over him.

I hit Jonah's hand as my transmitter speaks.

"Let me go."

"Give me a second to explain," he says.

"Jonah, I swear if you don-"

"You can't go on that assignment," he says,

interrupting me as he pulls me into a storage cupboard. He locks the door.

"I can and I will. Amy chose me."

"Doesn't matter that Amy chose you. This is a safety thing. You need to go to Amy's office and tell her you've changed your mind."

I scowl at him. *"No, I earnt that assignment. I put in the hours, and I've done the training. I'm going on that assignment."*

He shrugs and runs a hand through his hair. "Don't say I didn't warn you."

"I didn't ask you to warn me. Next time, mind your own business."

He yanks the door open and storms out. I roll my eyes and shake my head, knowing that this is typical Jonah behaviour. He's a team player until a leader is needed, and that's when he shows his true colours.

I step out of the cupboard and head in the opposite direction, making a beeline for the gymnasium. I completed my usual duties before the meeting as a just-in-case. Besides, after meeting with Amy tomorrow, my days will be filled with training so there'll be little time for getting my duties done.

Once I reach the gymnasium, I stretch and warm up. I practise routine drills, run three miles on the running machine before joining in with a synchronised movement class.

Once I feel satisfied and my body aches, I call it a day and head back to my accommodation.

"Heard you got the Observatory job," says my roommate, Mila, as I collapse on my bed.

"Hard work pays off," I say.

"Promise me you'll be careful."

"I promise."

CHAPTER THREE

At eight thirty, I collect my breakfast tray and join Mila at our usual table.

"When's your meeting?" she asks.

"In half an hour."

"Better eat quickly then, you're missing all of your badges." She points to the flap of fabric attached to my uniform.

"I put them on this morning before coming here," I think as I look down, and sure enough, I hadn't put them on. *"Shit."*

"You can't go into an official meeting without your badges."

I roll my eyes. *"I know that."*

Each of us earns badges, a bit like military medals, depending on years of service, successful assignments and rank. I have six badges in total; a five year service, three assignment based ones and my ranks of soldier and undercover operative. I completed the undercover training late last year and have yet to be sent on such a job. But the Observatory Aerimar job will change that.

I finish my breakfast before dumping my tray at the collection table. I sprint back to my room, bursting through the door and snatching up the long pin that holds my badges. I open the clasp with shaky hands, noting that I need to be at Amy's office in ten minutes. The second the pin in locked into the clasp, I jump back into the corridor before barrelling into the lift, just as the doors are closing.

"Cutting it a bit close." I turn and see Jonah leaning up against the back wall of the lift.

"Shut up, Jonah."

"Hope you have a good meeting."

I roll my eyes, imagining that I'm allowed to wrap my hands around his throat and strangle him.

"I can practically hear you thinking about murdering me."

"Haven't you anything better to do than follow

me around?"

"No."

The lift takes us to the floor -3 before the doors open and I'm out of there like a shot. I reach Amy's office just as she opens the door. I stand to attention, saluting her.

"Come on in," she says, gesturing to her office.

I stop saluting and step into the office, taking a seat as she shuts the door.

"Before we start, I want to double check that you still want to take on the assignment," she asks as she takes a seat opposite me.

"I still want to do it."

She nods with a smile. "We'll spend today going through all the information you'll need for the assignment."

I nod.

"As you know, the whole point of the job is to retrieve a box of Aerimar stones. This box of stones are different to the ones we normally use to power the base."

"What do you mean?"

"The box you need to get is full of ancient ones.

It's possible that these ancient versions of the stones predate the creation of this country. They were harvested from the cliff faces that sit just below the surface of the sea. It's not new knowledge that Aerimar stones could be linked to ancient ruins below the palace, but the only way we will be able to tell is by testing them against our samples."

"Has the Higher Power accessed the ruins?"

"No, not yet. It seems he doesn't know that the stones could be capable of activating the ruins. That's why it's important we get hold of them as quickly as possible."

I nod. *"What makes the ruins so important?"*

"They offer the perfect line into the palace if we try to take back control. The palace would give us a good amount of vantage over the Higher Power. At the moment we've been working on taking control of critical businesses and lower risk buildings. But for now, our main objective is to gain access to those ruins."

"Okay. Where are they being kept?"

"Underneath the astronomy exhibit." She makes her chair spin 180 degrees to the cabinet behind her.

She grabs a roll of blue paper before spinning back around. "This is a map of the second and third floors of the Observatory. Just like this place, the floors go down instead of up. The top floor is museum artefacts and exhibits. We'll send you in just after opening, and my team that works there will hide you until closing."

"Will I be taking equipment with me?" I ask as she hands me the map.

"You'll be going in mostly unarmed. I have Nix working on concealed weapons. It's something that we'll need in the future if checking procedures tighten, so you'll be working with a couple of her prototypes."

"What do the prototypes look like?"

"They look like everyday objects. I haven't seen the final designs yet, but I've been told they're coming together really well."

We move on to the blueprints that she grabs from the side of her desk. She rolls them out over her desk. She talks me through the three separate routes that I could take to get to the box. They vary in complexity, with route two being the simplest. She points out every single camera and every doorway that's being guarded by a Warden. I'm shown pictures of the staff members who will help hide me once I'm there and where to find them upon entry.

Amy gives me the outfit I'm going to be wearing. A combat type trouser with a jumper and heavy duty boots. It's the typical fashion these days, suits and smart work attire stopped being something people wore once the Higher Power shut down office jobs. I bag up the outfit and shove it into the rucksack Amy's also given me. It's full of pockets and zips where I can hide all sorts of equipment, and a large main pocket to keep the box in once I secure it.

Once we finish in the office, we walk to where Nix has been working. She's welding when we get there and doesn't notice us at first. But when she does, she stands to attention.

"How are the prototypes coming along?" asks Amy as she examines the table of items.

"They're coming along really well. I'm just putting the finishing touches on the last one."

"Would you mind showing us?"

"Not at all. Over here we have a selection of pen models that will successfully conceal a collapsible dagger."

Nix takes us through each design, showing us how the daggers blade folds in on itself before fitting neatly into the outer casing of the pen.

"Tomorrow you'll start training. Mark will meet you at half eight in the training rooms. You'll run simulations and run drills. Nix will then come and show you how to use the concealed weapons."

"Eight thirty in the training rooms. Got it."

"I'm glad you accepted this assignment. I can't think of anyone more suited to a job like this," Amy says as we arrive back at her office.

"Thank you for the opportunity. I won't let you down."

She nods. "Rest up, these next few days are going to be intense."

"Yes, Leader," I say, saluting her before we part ways.

Instead of heading back to my room, I take a detour toward our Chapel. I take a seat on one of the pews and prepare to say a prayer to the gods looking down on us. To pray for protection and good will until this assignment is over.

CHAPTER FOUR

I arrive at the training rooms bang on half eight to find Mark waiting for me. We shake hands before he welcomes me inside.

I've been in the shared training rooms many times before, but Mark is a private trainer who's reserved for special assignment training.

He's set the whole room up with equipment that will come in handy with helping me prepare. As we walk around the room, I take in all of the equipment. Some of them are pieces I've never seen before, which means Mark has had them custom made.

It feels daunting to be in a room with so much equipment that it makes a feeling of doubt settle in the pit of my stomach. I begin to doubt my ability to do anything as I take in all of the equipment and Mark must sense that. He reassures me that there's no reason to be concerned about the equipment. That the specific needs of this assignment don't require all of the large pieces, nor any of the intimidating weapons that line the walls. He tells me I will be fine, and I believe him.

I pull on my leg warmers before we start the warmup. We stretch, both standing and on the floor before moving onto running laps of the room. We jog four laps before picking up the pace to a steady run. We run another four laps before heading over to the crash mats. He then has me run through a series of basic hand to hand combat drills. When he calls time on the warmup, I pull off my knee warmers and the thin, exercise-friendly cardigan. I leave them folded neatly on the bench.

"I want you to do a slow run of the course. Just to get a feel of what you're going to be doing," he says as he walks us to the first piece of equipment.

I slowly run every single piece of equipment. Mark guides me through ones I've not seen before, and I power through the ones I know how to do. When I reach the end, Mark has me break for some water before having me do it again.

We do the same routine four times before we break for lunch. I thought we'd be eating with everyone else, but Mark hands me an identical tub of freshly prepared salad. Lettuce, shredded carrot, raisins, thinly sliced potatoes and some kind of dipping sauce that Mark claims is good for easing muscle burn. And goddamn does my whole body burn. Clearly I haven't been putting time into the right areas of training when I'm by myself.

After letting lunch digest, and a guided talk on keeping my calm during an assignment like this one, Mark has me do some light stretches. Then we move on to testing my flexibility when it comes to climbing oddly shaped walls or furniture.

"Why is this relevant?" I ask as I try to scale a wall with a curved top.

"Because the Observatory has surfaces like this. It's partly a museum and partly whatever the Higher Power is hiding underneath. Nothing about this building is normal. Now keep going, we're not moving on until you've successfully scaled the wall." I groan and we don't move on for half an hour when I finally manage to find the right grip to haul myself up and over the wall.

After that, we move onto practising with the fake daggers that Mark has neatly lined up on their wall mounts. This is by far my favourite part of the day because I specialised in weapons training. He has me running drills with them, repetitive movements until it feels like my arms might fall off. Once we finish, I feel good, the deep burn in my muscles acting as proof that I worked hard today.

"Get some sleep, tomorrow will be worse," he says as I pack up my water bottle and warm-up outfit.

"Can't wait."

"Nix will also join us tomorrow and we'll put her new weapons to the test."

I get back to my room and flop onto the bed, not even bothering to take my rucksack off. I lay face down, resting my sore body until Mila comes out of our shared bathroom. She peels me off the bed, demanding that I get in the shower.

I don't know how long I'm in the shower for, but I don't care as the feeling of the water on my skin is the most relaxing feeling in the world. The warm water from the shower has my muscles loosening just enough that I feel like I can move normally again.

"How was training?"

"Unbelievable. But good."

"Think you can make it to the dining hall for dinner or do you want me to bring you something back?"

"Thank you, but if I stay here I think I'll seize up."

"Come on then." She pulls me up from where I'm sitting on the edge of my bed, and she doesn't let go until we reach the dining hall.

As we wait in line, I feel someone stand extremely close behind me. They stand so close that I can feel their breath on the parting of my plaits. Turning my head, I see Jonah standing behind me, his hands shoved in his pockets and his eyes locked onto my face.

"I hear training started today," he murmurs.

"It did."

"Have fun?"

"Yes."

"Have you thought about what I said the other

day?"

"No."

"It'll be your funeral."

"Oh well, better to die in active service than be a coward."

He doesn't say anything more before storming off.

"What's his problem?" Mila asks as she hands me a tray.

"He's a grade A asshole. That's his problem."

※

Eight - oh - clock rolls around far too quickly.

After the beating my body took yesterday during training, I'm not really looking forward to doing it all again today. But I at the same time, I'm excited to be getting my hands on the actual weapons Nix has made for me.

Today's breakfast is one of my favourites. Buttered toast with tomato and a poached egg. It's my favourite mix they do, while Mila's is a bit of a love it or hate it mix. Buttered toast, spinach and grated cheese. Not quite my type of breakfast toppings but she swears by it.

"Ready for today?"

"No. My body is screaming at me, but there's no time for rest."

"Well, as long as you don't pass out from exhaustion."

"Guess we'll find out." I glance at my watch and find that it's eight twenty five. *"Gotta go, enjoy your mutant toast."*

"Shut up."

I grab my water bottle on the way to the training room and meet Mark outside.

"Ready for another day?"

"Yes."

"Good, Nix will be here shortly with the weapons so let's get warmed up."

We repeat the same warm up as yesterday. Four jogging laps, four fast laps and then hand to hand combat practice.

"Good morning," says Nix.

"Morning Nix. Are they in the bag?" Mark asks as he takes hold of the bag.

"Yep. I was told to run both of you through how they work before supervising the use of them in case any adjustments need to be made."

"Sounds good. Keres, take this one and get familiar with it. We start in five," he orders as he hands me the pen shaped casing.

I turn it over in my hand, looking curiously at how the dagger handle and blade fits into the pen casing.

"Can you show me how it works?" I ask Nix.

"Sure." She comes over to where I'm standing and takes the weapon from me.

"The blade folds in on itself and the nib of the pen is actually the point of the blade. It was hard to construct but I managed to do it in such a way that when you push this button at the top, the handle and blade will pop out of the casing."

"That's so cool. How long did it take you to figure it out?"

"Longer than I would have liked. But once I got the basic mechanism working it took two or three days to fit everything together for the first prototype."

"Right, let's begin," Mark calls, interrupting our

conversation.

For the rest of the morning, we practise arming the blade after the casing comes off. We practise possible scenarios that could happen during the job. We run through them until we're red in the face and panting.

After we finish letting our lunch digest, we move to the simulation room that's attached to the training room. I make myself familiar with the layout of the Observatory. I note every exit, every entrance and every fire escape. I make sure I know my way around the different exhibits. Seeing the layout in a semi-realistic makes me feel a lot more confident.

And then Amy comes bearing bad news.

"We've had to bring the timeline forward. I know you were meant to get a week's worth of training but you're going to have to make do with what you've already had. Tomorrow you need to go to medical to get all the tests done before you, Tina and James head over to the Observatory."

"Is something wrong?" I ask, curious as to why the date has been brought forward.

"Not wrong, just tense. There's a lot of

movement around the Capital City so I'm not taking any chances. Get some sleep, tomorrow will be a long day of prep."

"Yes Leader."

CHAPTER FIVE

Medical exams. A requirement for every member before they set off on their assignment. Normally, members just have an annual check-up, but it's important to Amy that everyone she sends on an assignment is in top condition, so pre-assignment check-ups are mandatory.

"Good morning Keres, here for a pre-assignment check?" Bailey, my favourite nurse, asks as I shut the door.

"You bet. Are you going to be my nurse today?"

"No, sorry. Madison's working on pre-assignments today."

I nod and lean against the front desk.

"You know, I had a really nice evening with you the other night."

"So did I. Maybe we could do it again when you get back?"

"That sounds like a very good idea."

"Good. Also gives you a reason to make sure you come back safe."

I smile at her and squeeze her hand before taking the clipboard she's left on the counter. I take a seat in the waiting area and fill in the forms before Madison calls my name.

I follow her into the exam room and take a seat on the bed.

"We'll start with a blood and a urine test before moving onto the physical exams. Sound good?"

"Fine by me."

Madison has me roll up my sleeve and she prepares to take two vials of blood. She does it quickly while asking me questions about my lifestyle.

Am I eating regularly? *Yes*.

Am I staying hydrated? *Yes*.

Do I have a regular sleep schedule? *Sort of.*

Once that's done, she gives the vials to Bailey who takes them to be rushed through at the lab.

She then has me do the urine test before we start

the first physical exam. That entails checking for lumps, bumps, strains, bruises and muscle mass. I pass with flying colours before she attaches me to a machine that measures the rhythms of my heart. Then she attaches the same stickers to my head. Once that test has finished, Madison moves me over to the physical exam lab. She sets up a running machine which she uses to measure my vital signs while I exert myself. She has me run for three minute intervals with one minute rests in between.

"Looks like all of your tests are coming back fine. You're healthy and fit." She sits down at her desk and starts typing at the computer.

"Give this letter and form to Amy. You're medically cleared for the assignment." She prints out the two pages and hands them to me.

"Thank you, Madison."

"You'll be given your Medi-kit before you leave."

"See you then," I say, taking my papers and leaving the exam room.

I head straight to Amy's office to give her the papers. She thanks me before I head to the dining hall to have a late lunch with Mila.

"Ready for tomorrow?"

"More than ready."

CHAPTER SIX

I roll over in bed and look at the clock on my nightstand.

4:00 am.

After a late lunch with Mila yesterday, I skipped my individual training slot in the gym and headed back to my room instead. I showered and changed into my pyjamas. I set my alarm for quarter past four, but since I'm already awake, I roll out of bed. Extremely ungraceful might I add.

I grab the rucksack Amy gave me and pour the clothes, that I'd shoved in there, onto the bed. I change quietly, not wanting to disturb Mila. Once changed, I neatly fold my pyjamas before heading into the bathroom. I wash my face, brush my teeth and brush my hair thoroughly before plaiting it down onto my left shoulder. I exit the bathroom, grab the rucksack from the bed and quietly leave.

Before heading to the garage, I swing by the dining hall and grab one of the premade oat pots. It's a standard pre-assignment meal. It's not too heavy, and it's not too light. We can have a mixture of fruit pots with it and yoghurt if we choose it. I swipe a spoon from the cutlery tray and start eating as I walk to the garage.

The majority of the base is covered in shadows, the artificial night and day system working well. The base always looks spooky at night, probably something to do with the way the metal creaks as it supports the ground above us. And we always know when someone on the surface is using heavy machinery. The metal walls around us rumble like thunder as the machinery vibrates it all. The first time I heard it, it was terrifying. But I'm used to it now. It's become comforting to hear, to know that we are all still here, completely undiscovered and driving the Higher Power mad.

I push open the door to the garages with my back as I eat a spoonful of my breakfast.

"Good morning," I say as I spot Tina sitting on one of the benches.

"Morning," she mumbles through a mouthful of oats.

"Ready for today?" I ask, taking a seat on the bench opposite her.

"Yep. Not done a job like this for a while so I'm hoping all the work I did with Jackie paid off."

I nod. *"You'll be fine. I think you've done more assignments than most people in this base."*

"You're too kind." Tina has been here from the very start. She's Amy's stepcousin, and by far the most experienced out of all of us. She's been working on assignments since she was twelve, taking part in low impact and low risk jobs until she was eighteen. That's when she started taking on higher impact assignments before training to work undercover. Tina's a role model for all of us, and to be doing this assignment with her is an honour.

We finish our breakfasts in silence before placing the tubs in the kitchen shoot. Come the general breakfast service at 8am, all reusable tubs will be released down the shoot tunnel and straight into the sinks in the kitchen.

I look at the light above the kit room door and see that it has turned green, meaning that we can now grab whatever equipment we need. Tina grabs her items while I scan the shelves, admiring the equipment that is kept in here. Like Amy said, I will be going in without large weapons, so the garage mechanics didn't label anything for me to take.

"Here, this is for you," Tina says. I turn to look at her and see that she is holding out a signal blocker.

"Why do I need that?"

"For you rucksack. You have Nix's concealed weapons, no?"

I nod.

"Then you'll need this to trick the security sensors that you've no metal items in your bag."

I nod, taking the device. *"Thank you."*

Bailey pops in moments after we retake our seats on the benches. She's still in her pyjamas and her hair is lightly tousled. She looks cute like this, and I can't help but smile at her. She walks to Tina first, passing her a Medi-pack before giving me mine.

"Be safe out there," Bailey says as she takes hold

of one of my hands and squeezes it.

"Always."

"Promise me."

"I promise, especially since we're going out when I get back," I say, placing a chaste kiss on her cheek. She smiles and looks down at her feet.

"Good luck," she says before walking away.

We sit in silence again. I use the time to check my bag. To familiarise myself with the layout of the hidden pockets just in case. I stuff the Medi-pack right at the bottom and zip it up just as Amy walks into the garage. James follows closely behind her.

"Good morning everyone," she beams. "I wanted to come wish you all luck on this assignment. I believe in you, and I picked you because you were the right fit for this."

"Thank you, Amy," Tina says. James and I nod in agreement.

"Well, I'll let the three of you go. You'll be heading out in one of the organisation's official registered vehicles. I've reserved a parking space at the Observatory for you. 45B, Level 2. Good luck."

The garage door opens and the three of us head

toward the vehicle. James gets in the driver's seat; Tina gets in the passenger seat, and I hop in the back. James starts the car and pulls out of the garage. In the rear-view mirror I see Amy wave us off.

I take a deep breath and run through the plan in my head one last time.

CHAPTER SEVEN

We pull into our reserved parking space at half seven.

Two hours and forty five minutes in a car and my legs feel worse than they did after Mark's crash course training. I take my seatbelt off and stretch my legs across the two back seats.

"What time does the Observatory open?" James asks, his transmitter beeping.

"Nine," Tina tells him.

He huffs and I feel him shuffle in his seat. It's not ideal, being parked out here for so long. We could draw all kinds of attention to ourselves. Anyone who has a vehicle, owned or rented, must register it and have access to a parking space. A parking space which they can rent or buy from the Higher Power's Traffic Sector. So parking somewhere else isn't an option. We can only hope that we don't draw a Warden's attention and get asked to submit to a spot check.

∗

At quarter past nine I leave our vehicle and head round to the front entrance.

I pull my ticket from my bag and present it to the Warden at the front gate. They examine it before handing it back and allowing me through the gates. I head up the marble carved stairs and upon reaching the top, I discover more Wardens. Though this time, they are standing next to whole body scanners. I knew that security would be tightening at public buildings like this one, but only now has it dawned on me how overly cautious the Higher Power is being.

I take off my bag and hand it to the closest Warden.

"Step through the scanner," the Warden orders.

I do so. The scanner lights up green as I step out and the Warden hands me my bag without issue. I let out a deep breath. Adrenaline is running rampant through my body, and it takes a moment to gain control of myself as I head to the first exhibit.

The Turning Planet. A near life-like replica, in look, not size, of the unnamed planet visible from the ground. It trails just behind the moon during its orbit and is a sight to behold. No one knows why the planet sits where it does, no one knows what its purpose either. But for most, it's become something to pray to, something to send our wishes and deepest thoughts to in search of comfort and answers.

I do a full circle of the exhibit, briefly stopping at each signpost to skim over the facts before heading to the exit. On the way out I bump into a staff member. Our hands brush as they pass me a scrap of paper. I carefully manoeuvre the paper up and into my sleeve before heading to the bathroom.

I duck into the first stall, smiling briefly at the woman standing in front of the mirror. I lock the door before taking a seat on the closed toilet lid. Pulling the paper from my sleeve, I open it as quietly as I can.

4pm, second floor atrium, south corner.

I commit the words to memory before opening the toilet lid and tossing the paper into the water. I press the flush button and close the lid. I straighten myself, making a little bit of shuffling noise so as to not arouse suspicion from the woman outside.

"Busy day out there today," she says as I start washing my hands. I glance at her in the mirror and see she's in uniform.

"Certainly looks that way," I say to her as I turn off the tap. I grab a paper towel and dry my hands before leaving, not wanting to let her get too good of a look at me.

I head to the planetarium, a large, darkened room off to the right of the Turning Planet. I pass Tina and James, the two of them walking hand in hand. Tina wildly points to different things, enthusiasm lacing her voice. They're going to be keeping the Wardens on their toes by getting too close to the exhibits and finding themselves in places they aren't meant to be. That way, they won't be looking at me or anyone else, their orders will be to focus on the couple making quite the racket.

For now, I just need to blend into the crowd and

act as natural as possible.

※

At 4pm, I go to the south corner of the second floor atrium. A member of the Rebellion meets me and takes me to a side room. The staff member, who I now know as Simone, tells me to sit behind a load of plastic tarpaulin.

"The likelihood of someone coming in here is slim since its under construction," she says as she moves some of the tarpaulin so that it hides me better.

"Thanks," I tell her as she heads to the door.

"Stay quiet and I'll see you at closing."

I sit in that room for two and a half hours with nothing but my thoughts to keep me company. Thankfully, Simone comes back bang on closing and lets me know that the Wardens are done checking the vents. That means it's time to head into the vents and inner walls. When the building was originally constructed, the builders left small corridors within the walls so that they could easily get around the construction site. It prevented them from walking over areas that were filled with high value furniture and items. They never filled the gaps in, which makes it easier for me to get around now that the place has closed.

It doesn't take me long to find the room in which the stones are being kept. I slow my breathing as I watch through one of the conveniently drilled peep holes. I patiently wait for the Wardens to leave the room. Each room is checked top to bottom before the internal Warden guards clock out for the night. Three night duty Wardens will then patrol the building until sunrise tomorrow, and thanks to Simone, I know I'll have three minutes and thirty seconds to get the box and get back inside the wall.

As the Warden comes closer to the wall I'm standing behind, I duck down and carefully open my rucksack. I pull out the daggers hidden in the seams and put them on the floor. I rezip the bag and swing it back onto my shoulders. Then I pick up the weapons and place them in their designated hiding spaces in my outfit.

As soon as the Warden steps out of the room, I push open the concealed door and head straight for the box. This room is a storage of sorts for old objects and rare artefacts, just like the stones. Each item has a labelled podium, so it only takes a quick dive across the room to get to the box. I swing my rucksack from one arm, yanking the zip open. I shove the box into my bag and quickly zip it up.

Just as I slip back through the door, I hear a Warden walk into the room. They must catch sight of the back of my boot as a shout has me running straight down the inner corridor. I scramble into the vent that takes me back to the empty room. I practically fall out of it before barrelling through the folded tarps. I burst through the door and sprint down the main hallway in an attempt to lose the two Wardens who've also spotted me.

As much as I hate to say it, right now would be a good time to have Jonah running next to me. He's a reserve Warden, one of Amy's favourite career paths to recruit. He'd know exactly where all of the hotspots for escaping would be.

I fly down the stairs and dive straight into the atrium. I duck and jump around the benches and cases that line the floor. I take the next door on my left just as I catch sight of a Warden advancing on me from the right. It lets me into a passageway. I sprint down it, briefly letting myself take in the marble arches that stretch high above me, and the windowless frames that give me an uninterrupted view of the night sky.

None of this route was on the simulation tests I did. None of this was anywhere in the blueprints I looked at with Amy during our meeting. For all I know I could be running into a place that has no way out.

As I make my way down the next set of stairs, the pounding of Warden boots thump against the floor above me. I crash through a wooden door and start taking two stairs at a time, quickly descending a spiralling staircase. I exit at the next available floor and start sprinting. I run in a straight line before taking various rights and lefts.

Once I feel like I'm far enough away, I slow down just enough to be able to deal with the stitch in my side. I lean against the wall and take deep breaths. I push my hand against my side, willing the pain to go away.

The pounding of boots has me wishing I worked

faster on getting the box out of that room. I could've put the box in my bag once I was safely behind the walls. A stupid mistake.

A loud shout has me diving into the nearest room, slamming the door carelessly behind me. The pain subsides a little, so I take stock of the room in front of me. Black walls with white spots decorating them like freckles. A shelf to my left and a tarp covering part of the wall in front of me. On impulse, I tug on the tarp. I half expect it to reveal a painting from a time long gone, instead, I find a dark abyss. I discard the tarp and step toward the gaping hole in the wall. Could it be a way out?

The gap in the wall has jagged and sharp edges, dangerous enough to severely hurt someone if they weren't looking where they were going. I step closer, shivering at the cold breeze that hits me. Two walls, a ceiling and a beam. No floor though, which sets off all kinds of alarm bells in my mind.

A blade swoops across the space, centimetres from the tips of my boots. It slices through the air before disappearing into the opposite wall. A second blade a few metres away follows the same movements. Deciding that I want to get out of this alive, I head back to the door and step back into the corridor.

The hallway is silent, the only exception being the sound of my boots echoing against the stone floor. It feels like I've been walking for years, but then I notice a crack in the floor. It's shallow, but decently wide. The further I walk, the further it seems to stretch. I bend down next to it and run my finger over it. A soft breeze brushes against the pad of my finger. I lift my finger away before making a fist and rapping my knuckles against the floor. The ground underneath me is hollow.

There's another floor.

I stop crouching and begin to follow the crack. Ten paces down the hallway and the crack begins to veer off to the right before trailing up the wall. I follow it all the way across the ceiling until it falls back onto the left wall of the hallway.

Then it stops.

I run my finger over where the crack stops, and the pad of my finger brushes a rough patch of metal. I bring my face closer, squinting through the shadows.

A tiny button has been half concealed in the wall. The area where they've inserted the mechanism to whatever it opens has been roughly sanded down.

Deciding to try my luck, I press the button.

"In for a penny," I mutter to myself as the wall clicks open.

A small breeze brushes over me, the hairs on my arms stand on end. I peer into the space, but I can't see anything. Another dark abyss. I move further through the doorway but the toe of my shoe dangles over an edge. My hand shoots out and grabs onto a metal pole just as two lights click. With better visibility, I look down below and see a metal staircase.

"Found you."

I jump back, staring down the hallway. A Warden stands mere metres away, only pausing to gauge my reaction. I don't give him the chance to get any closer as I launch myself down the staircase, my hands skimming over the metal bannisters to keep me steady.

I hear the Warden following me. The sheer force of his boots on the metal stairs has it wobbling, proving that this is a temporary entrance. A badly built temporary entrance which means that all of this underground space is new. Amy was right, the Higher Power is hiding something down here.

I fly off the bottom step, crashing into the wall opposite. I take a second to collect myself before jogging down the corridor to my left. It's dimly lit, but a bright light in the distance catches my attention. And so does the scattering of doors every ten steps or so. Curiosity creeps up my spine but heavy footsteps behind me have me drawing the pen casing and activating the blade.

I turn and watch the Warden fall off the last step, stumbling clumsily. He scans both sides of the passageway before spotting me.

"Run again, and I'll cut off your feet," he sneers as he draws his sword.

"You're going to have to catch me first," I taunt.

I square my shoulders and wait for him to come to me. In this kind of situation it's always better to be the one standing still, rather than being the one to attack first. I want to gauge his stance and measure his patience. It doesn't take long but he does exactly what

I want him to. He lunges toward me, wildly swinging his sword. I take a step back, leaning to avoid the blade. He swings his arm too hard, and the blade catches the wall, briefly sticking into the stone so I take my chance. I swing my dagger, aiming for his neck. It takes a second to register that he's injured before he's stumbling backwards, clawing and grasping at his throat. Gurgling instead of screaming. I watch and wait to make sure he dies. I can't risk someone finding him and attempting to bring him back.

As he stops moving, two more Wardens enter the hallway. I don't move. I don't even breathe. I simply observe them from the corner of my eye. As the first Warden steps forward, I notice the sash she's wearing. It indicates she's a Captain. She wastes no time in charging at me. She does the same as the Warden before her and swings her sword at me. I dodge the attack, turning my body to the side before stabbing my dagger into her side, twisting as I pull it out. She screams, randomly slashing her sword. She gets me on the arm, barely grazing the top layers of skin before I return with a deep slash to her upper arm. She stumbles and slides down the wall.

The second Warden is a Lieutenant. Highly trained in hand to hand combat and psychological warfare. Smart people who don't let themselves be tricked easily during a fight. So I resort to taunting him. Cocking my head to the left and smiling. Goading him to come for me, to attack first. But he doesn't move and that makes impatience run up my spine. The adrenaline of beating two Wardens gets to me as I lunge at him. I'm ready to strike his throat, to take him down in one move but a hand gripping my ankle stops me. The hand pulls and I drop my dagger, bracing my hands in front of me before rolling onto my back. I gasp as the corners of the box dig into my back. I look down and see the Captain dragging herself on top of me. I've got limited movement as she's resting on my legs, but as soon as she gets to my waist, I bend my knees and bring them up and into her stomach. She groans and rolls off of me.

I take my chance and grab my dagger. I lodge it in the Captain's throat. In the brief time she's still alive she rams her own dagger into my thigh. My transmitter screams in response to the pain coursing through my leg. I pull my blade from her neck after she stops moving just as the Lieutenant lifts me up by my armpits. He lifts me just enough so that he can open my rucksack. I feel him take the box out before unceremoniously dropping me. My head collides with the concrete and a blinding pain ebbs behind my eyes.

"I've not battled a mute with such fighting spirit for quite some time. You've proven a challenging adversary. Unfortunately though, you're not quite good enough to get out of this alive," he boasts as he swipes at me with his sword.

I move away from him with all the strength I have left. I drag myself up to the wall, leaning against it panting and sweating in pain. He crouches down in front of me, his hand coming and gripping my face, his fingers painfully digging into my skin. I try to look away, but he forces me to look at him.

"Any last words?"

I weakly shake my head, struggling against hold. I feel my body shutting down, dizziness spots my vision and nausea climbs my throat.

"Goodb–" I cut him off, thrusting my dagger into his heart with all of the strength I have left. He gulps and chokes before falling backwards, thudding against the floor.

My transmitter groans and screams as I get onto my knees. I crawl over to the Lieutenant's body and pull out my dagger. Sitting back on my heels, I wipe the blood on the jumper. I grab the box of stones that's laying haphazardly underneath him. I get back onto my hands and knees and crawl over to the opposite wall.

As I reach it, I drop onto my right side before managing to pull myself up. I gently rest my back against the curve in the wall in an attempt to support myself. But it doesn't work, and I slouch down. My chin rests on my chest as my eyes struggle to stay open.

CHAPTER EIGHT

My eyes flutter open and the first thing to hit me is the metallic smell of blood.

I know I'm covered in it, and the three bodies across from me are covered in it too. I can practically taste it which makes me gag, and the movement from that makes my body hurt.

My leg is throbbing. I look down and see that I'm sitting in a growing puddle of my own blood. The blade that the Captain stuck in my leg is in there deep. It twinges with every movement, and I know for a fact I'll be in rehabilitation for months when I get out of here.

I take a deep breath and take stock of what I have. Three more blades, water, four cereal bars, a Medi-pack and a box of stones. Not great in the grand scheme of things, but for now, they'll have to do.

I lean forward and take my bag off, fighting to pull it from where its wedged between my back and wall. I haphazardly unzip it and root around for the Medi-pack. In the end, frustration at not being able to find what I want gets the better of me, so I turn the bag upside down and emptying it onto the concrete. I open the Medi-pack. Carefully, I place down the sterile equipment on its plastic boarding before taking a look at the dagger. It's in there deep, and the any amount of damage it did going in will double when I pull it out.

I press the wound and groan in pain. The skin around the wound smarts, and it takes everything in me not to scream.

I reach for the roll of gauze. I unwind it, ripping a large amount off and pinching it between my fingers. I place it around the blade and squeeze. I let out a choked sound as my breath gets caught in my throat.

Collect yourself, relax. You've been trained for incidents like this.

I collect myself before gripping the handle with my free hand and start pulling the blade out very gently. I breathe in short puffs of air as the blade drags along the inside of my thigh, scraping muscle and flesh. My transmitter screams and tears stream down my face. The squelch as the blade leaves my leg has me gagging again, nausea rising up my throat. I lean to the side, heaving and coughing. It's takes a few moments but once I regain control of myself, I pack the wound.

I slouch back against the wall again, my chin back resting on my chest and my eyes fluttering shut. Dizziness starts to take hold again and my mind starts slipping. It slips in and out of a place of peace and tranquillity. To a place where my whole body feels like liquid, and there's not a single ounce of pain. A place anywhere other than here.

I feel myself slip to the side. My back grinds against the rough concrete before my forehead comes to rest against the cold floor.

Comfy. Cold. Soothing.

I don't want to move, but I know I have too. I let out a long sigh as I force myself to roll onto my back. I lay still, my hips twisted to the side as I try to regain control of the pain. It's almost blinding and for the briefest of moments I feel like giving up. I feel like resting here until someone finds me. A Warden can find me for all I care, at least I would get medical attention before they start an interrogation.

I let my eyes roll to the back of my head as my mind slips again. I'm no longer in a darkened passageway when I open my eyes. Instead, I'm lying in a park. My body is in the same position, but I'm out in the fresh air. I'm free and rays of sun are melting away the deep set chill from my bones. I see faint people– no, children. I hear their laughter and their pounding footsteps. Giggles that echo around the park. The echoes should get quieter, but they only get louder. They bounce around my head and it's loud, so, so, so loud. I move my hands to protect my head, but nothing ever comes crashing over me. The phantom sounds are hallucinations and I'm not in a park. I'm stuck in an underground passageway.

My eyes open and I stare at the ceiling. I won't die in this passageway. There's no way I'm going to die, not today at least.

I take a couple of deep breaths. I lift my legs so that my ankles are resting against the curve of the wall. I press the gauze harder against the wound. My head shoots up from the concrete at the sudden jolt of pain and a scream rips from my throat.

Fuck, that hurts.

I reach out to the side with my free hand and grabbing the rest of the gauze and a clean bandage. I lay the fabrics on my chest before taking out the sodden gauze. I chuck it onto the concrete before repacking it into the wound. Once I'm sure it isn't going to fall out, I grab the bandage and wind it tightly around my leg. I secure it with a bit of tape from the Medi-pack before letting my arms flop to the side.

Exhaustion bubbles inside of me, and the urge to sleep invades my mind. But I can't stop now, So I roll onto my left shoulder, my legs sliding down the wall. They hit the ground with such a thud that you'd think my boots were lined with weights. I groan at the pain that runs along my thigh before carefully bringing myself into the sitting position. I crawl over to my bag and start packing everything away, the remains of the Medi-pack, the cereal bars, the stones and whatever else I dumped onto the floor.

I use the wall to help me stand up and I swing the rucksack over my shoulder. I stumble and land awkwardly on my right knee. I hiss at the burn of my skin skidding along the concrete. I take a second to centre myself before trying again. I haul myself up, and this time I stay upright. I take a step forward, using the wall as my guide.

As I walk, I decide my first stop won't be the staircase I used to get down here, it's going to be the blinding bright light at the end of the passageway. I start heading toward it, taking tiny, pigeon steps.

As my hand trails the wall, it brushes over metal and wood. I turn my head and find one of what looks to be many doors. This one is similar in appearance to the ones in the earlier hallway. I lean against it for a second before deciding to open it. I'm looking down at the ground when I step inside, and when I look up, I'm greeted by the most beautiful sight. In front of me stands a beautiful mountain range with a waterfall at the centre. Vibrant blue water cascades down it before crashing into a pool of the clearest water. The sky is an array of purples and pinks as the sun sets far beyond the mountains. Tall trees become skeletons

and a cool breeze sweeps past. I follow the waterfall
back to the pool. The water shimmers as it catches the
moonlight, and a faint smile works its way onto my
face. A landscape so beautiful, so different to the
actual ones of this world that I feel like I'm receiving
a gift. The gift of being able to witness such a
phenomenon.

"How did this get here?" I wonder.

This isn't something you can build with materials
from the natural land, nor from any man-made
materials. A passageway such as this tells me that the
Higher Power is experimenting with other worlds.
Worlds he shouldn't be able to get too.

Amy will be pleased with this discovery.

I step back into the passageway, closing the door
behind me. I carefully limp over to the next door.
Pulling it open, I gasp. Inside of this doorway is a
silver bridge that's covered in a thin layer of snow. It
sparkles like glitter as moon rays illuminate the
ground. Peeking out from under the snow are raised
patterns of flowers, stems and leaves. Bright silver
handrails line the bridge, each one intricately crafted
with floral patterns. It's truly mesmerising, and as I

continue to take in the details, the bridge becomes a leading line, and my eyes follow it to a beautiful temple. Architectural spires rise high into the midnight sky, becoming silhouettes as the moon rises behind them. Small candles flicker along the stone walls of the bridge. The whole place is like the home of cosmic royalty. It's stunning.

My chest becomes heavy as the doors of the temple call to me. I step onto the bridge and the snow swirls around my ankles. It's like it's trying to guide me, to drag me further down the bridge, but I stand still. I bend at the waist as I try to collect some of the snow. It's soft and cold, and when I brush it away it stains my skin like silver paint. It starts to burn so I quickly wipe it on my trousers.

The calls of the temple get louder, but I know I need to leave. I stumble back towards the door, tripping over the metal threshold. The door slams shut behind me and I slide down the front of it covered in snowy paint and dried blood.

Closing my eyes, I rest my head against the door. My whole body throbs and pulses with injury. I long for a comfy hospital cot and a warm blanket. I'm freezing cold, the kind of cold that you can feel in your bones. Thoughts of the base hit me hard, and I start to think about what might happen next. The possibility of what could come. The possibility that I'm going to die in this passageway, alone.

I rub my eyes, groaning in frustration. I have no way to contact Tina or James, these kinds of assignments work on radio silence and a carefully timed plan. When they go wrong, it's up to the individual in trouble to get themselves out. And right now, I don't think I'll get out at all. But footsteps echoing off the passageway walls brings me out of my thoughts. I quickly stumble to my feet.

A Warden.

They stand there, unmoving.

Then they take a step toward me, to which I respond by taking a step back. We continue this until I'm practically on the edge of the brightly lit room. The Warden stops two doors away and we stare at each other. Neither of us willing to make the first move.

They take another step forward.

"Keres?"

"Jonah."

"People were beginning to worry," he says as he takes a step closer. He shouldn't be here. I swallow thickly, not trusting him.

"What are you doing here?"

"I could ask you the same thing."

"I'm on my assignment."

"I know. I mean what are you doing down here?"

"I was chased." I gesture to the three dead Wardens on the floor.

"I can see that."

He takes another step, and I ready myself. I look at the way he's standing. The expression on his face.

"What are you doing here, Jonah?" I repeat.

He takes a deep breath before coming to stand right in front me, just close enough that our chests nearly touch.

"I can't let you leave with those stones."

CHAPTER NINE

I stare up at him, shocked.

"Jonah, don't tell m–"

He interrupts me. "Those stones are going to be vital to the Higher Power's next move, and I can't let you give them to Amy."

"Traitor."

"Give me the stones. I won't you ask again."

"Jonah," I warn, unsheathing my dagger.

He shakes his head. "I told you I wouldn't ask again."

He moves quickly, taking a blade from his uniform. I block him, managing to dislodge the knife. It falls over the edge and into the bright abyss beneath me.

I turn my back on him and head into the new

room. The floor is soft, my footsteps making no sound. It's a cloud, and I feel like I should be sinking into it, but I don't. Jonah uses my slight distraction to his advantage as his boot collides with my back. I crumple and my transmitter grumbles at the pain in both my back and the shock running through both my knees.

I push myself to sit on my backside and kick my legs out at him as he tries to restrain my hands. I catch him in the chest, making him stumble backwards. Not waiting for him to recover, I scramble to my feet and run. The adrenaline coursing through my veins keeps me going.

I'm not looking where I'm running and as I try to catch myself, I teeter on the edge of the cloud and inevitably fall off the edge. I freefall no more than twenty feet before landing on another. I scramble to my feet and start running again. I find the edge of the cloud and look down. Nothing underneath me.

"Keres," Jonah shouts. I look up and find him glaring down at me. I wish I could get further away, but my cloud is too low down. I'm at the very bottom of this room with no way up.

"Keres, if you come to me now, I'll make sure they spare you. You'd do well working for the Higher Power."

"Oh really? Or would I become a pet he can show off to his supporters? To show that he is capable of capturing rebels and making fools of them," I yell back just as my cloud starts to ascend. I'm shocked but I don't let it consume me as soon as I jump onto a new cloud and start running.

"Stop running," he yells, sounding slightly breathless.

I do stop running, but not because he told me too. My thigh is throbbing, each step is sending sharp pains across my thigh and into my knee. I glance down and see the bandage I put on earlier is completely soaked through with blood. How my leg is still working is beyond me, and I have to bend in the middle to try and catch my breath.

Jonah marches toward me, a new dagger in his right hand. It glints in the few rays of sun coming from behind the clouds, almost like it's winking at me. I can't stay still forever.

What can I do?

What can I do?

If this place is being fuelled by whatever magic the Higher Power has harvested from another world, maybe I can use it to my advantage. If I managed to make the cloud move upwards when I wished I had somewhere else to run too, maybe I could get it to do something else.

I move to the edge of the cloud, take a deep breath, close my eyes and raise my arms. I look to the sky and pray – no wish – that a cloud will catch me. And as I let myself go; a new cloud catches me. I sigh with relief, and when I open my eyes, I see Jonah bent over the side of his cloud, glaring down at me.

I think about being raised above him so that he can't get to me, and I send a prayer to the gods when my cloud begins to rise. It raises me up and out of Jonah's reach. In fact, it takes me higher than the cloudy edge that blocks off the rest of the room. I sit on my backside and face the mountain of clouds. When the top of the mountain cloud comes into view, I get a peek at what's being hidden behind it.

"Oh my god."

What I thought were rays of sun hitting Jonah's

dagger, turns out to be plumes of blue and red light. The vapours dance around me and my cloud, leaving a cool tailwind behind them. But I'm quickly distracted by the half planet hanging in the sky. It's huge and completely unmissable. Red veins spiral out from the centre, twisting and growing with each movement. I watch as the veins seem to be drawn to each other and they look to be building the planet. A planet is being born right in front of my eyes.

The Higher Power is building a new world.

My cloud jolts, making me wobble. The planet starts to disappear behind the cloud mountain, and I see I'm heading back to the passageway. Once there, I slide off the cloud and look back to find Jonah already making his way to me. He's not running, he's not even speed walking. He knows I won't get very far very quickly. I'm too injured for that. But I don't let that bother me as I run. And I don't stop until I find a divot in the side of the wall.

I tuck myself inside of it and try to bury my forehead in the wall. My body feels like it's finally shutting down. My vision dances with blurriness and I have to wedge the material of my jumper in my mouth as a distraction.

I wait for Jonah to pass by me, hoping that the divot provides enough cover. He does just that and once he's a step ahead of me, I limp out from my hiding spot and drive one of my daggers into his clavicle. He curses and falls to his knees. I start walking again, I make sure to bump him with my good leg as I walk past him. He curses and groans.

I feel like I've travelled miles, but a hand on my ankle has me falling like a breeze sweeping over a deck of cards.

"Give me. The stones," he pants as he pulls the dagger from his clavicle and sheaths it in his pocket.

He towers above me. I try to shove him, but he just grabs my wrists and slams them onto the ground next to my head. I grunt, weakly kicking with my good leg. But it seems like he was expecting it so he's ready to block it.

"Stop struggling."

"Get off me."

"Give me the stones then."

I bring my bad leg up and knee him in the stomach. He wasn't expecting it this time and groans as he rolls off me. My transmitter screams at the final jolt of pain that runs down my injured leg. I reach down to check the bandage and my hand comes back wet. I lay there weakly, blood smeared all over me, and a blinding headache beginning to pulse behind my eyes.

I have no more energy. My body won't respond, and I think my leg has finally gone. I can't feel it anymore. I try to wiggle my toes, but I can't even do that.

I'm going to die here, at the hands of Jonah. Tears start to leak from my eyes and curse myself for not being more careful.

I flick my eyes over to where Jonah landed and see him coming back over. He bends down and rolls me over. He opens my rucksack and takes out the box of stones, discarding it on the concrete. The only relief I feel is in my back, at the lack of hard wooden corners digging into my skin.

Jonah bends back down and picks me up bridal style. I lay there limply in his arms and all I can do is watch as he takes us closer to the clouds. He stops a step away from the edge before placing me down. He turns me around to face him. He holds onto me tightly, his arms around my waist taking my weight since I can't support myself anymore. I feel one of his hands move and then I jolt. Looking down at my stomach I find my own dagger protruding from my stomach, the same one that I stabbed him with.

"You should've just given me the stones," he says as he pulls out the dagger and he spins me round to face the clouds. He lets me fall to my knees as I fight to keep my eyes open.

"I'm sorry, Keres. But the Higher Power has been right all along, and I can't let you interfere with his plans."

"You're a dick," I sputter, red droplets of blood spraying out of my mouth.

"I know," he says as he uses his boot to push me off the ledge.

CHAPTER TEN

I fall for what feels like an eternity.

Then I hit soft cloud. It cradles me and I feel completely weightless. I feel safe as I give into the darkness that wants so desperately to take me away.

Tendrils of cloud start to wrap around me, pulling me further down. I feel my body become covered in goosebumps as I become part of the cloud.

I take a last look at the half planet, letting the image imprint in my mind as the darkness begins to take over.

ABOUT THE AUTHOR

A. Carys is a self-published author from Portsmouth, United Kingdom. Other than spending 90% of her day writing, she also loves to crochet, read, and take photos of her family's cats.

Printed in Great Britain
by Amazon